D1609371

This book is to highlight the beautiful hue of children and people of color.

Based on a true story.

This book is dedicated to:
Mrs. Majors,
my mommy, Recia Johnson,
and my grandmother, Dessie Chandler.

To my African, African American, Afro Latina, Albino, Caribbean, and Hispanic children, YOU can do anything you want, just believe.

ISBN: 978-1-7330802-0-0
Melanin Poppin': Mommy, Why is My Skin Tone Different Than Yours?

Proudly self-published through Divine Legacy Publishing,
www.divinelegacypublishing.com

Melanin Poppin':
Mommy, Why is My Skin Tone Different Than Yours?

Melanin - Urban Dictionary meaning

Noun: Melanin is ubiquitous in every entity on Planet Earth that has hue or color.

Melanin is the root of what gives color to skin, hair, eyes, plants, oil, animals, volcanoes, and everything imaginable that is creative and colorful. Melanin is 100% activated through sun contact with Black/ Indigenous peoples and 50 to 100% with those Hispanic and all other people of color.

This is Chrissy. She is 6 years old. Chrissy goes to daycare and gets to play with many different children. Some are Black. Some are White. Some are Hispanic.

One day, while playing with other children, Chrissy realizes everyone has different skin tones. Some are really light. Some are brown. Some are dark brown. Some are medium brown.

As the day ends, Chrissy looks at the other children's parents picking them up from daycare while she waits for her mommy.

Chrissy notices something quite different and says to the daycare teacher, Mrs. Sanchez, “I think my mommy is white.”

Startled by the comment, Mrs. Sanchez asks, “Why do you think that?”

Chrissy takes her 16-count crayon box out of her backpack and says, “I am brown like this crayon, while my mommy is lighter like this crayon. If mommy was Black, then wouldn’t she look like me?”

Mrs. Sanchez has never thought of this logic and waits for Chrissy's mother, Teresa, to pick her up to explain what she has discovered. When she arrives, Mrs. Sanchez pulls Teresa aside to explain the conversation that she and Chrissy shared.

In the car ride home Chrissy's mom asks, "Chrissy, what color am I?" Chrissy replies, "White". Teresa decides this is a good time to teach Chrissy about the word called MELANIN.

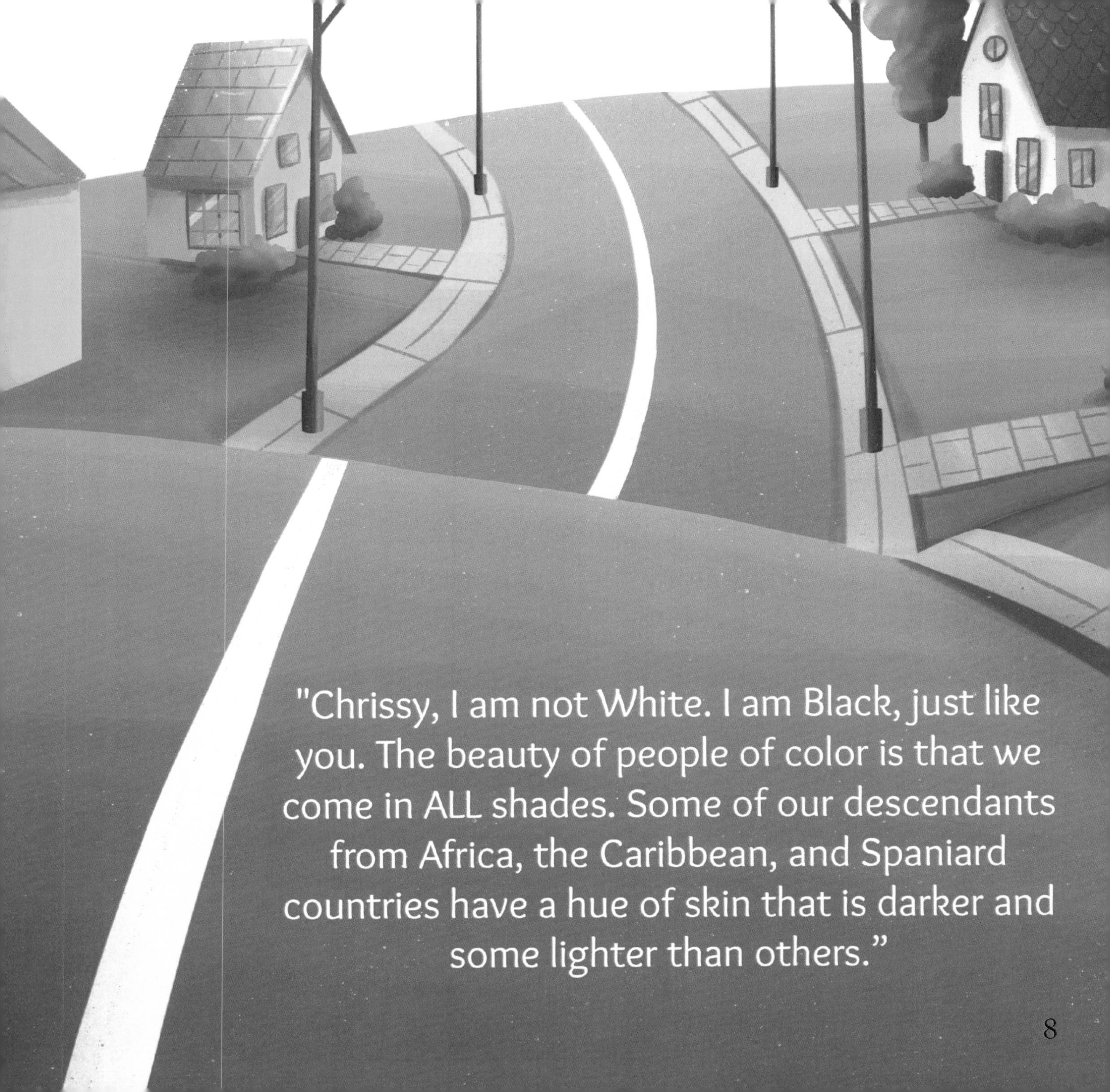

"Chrissy, I am not White. I am Black, just like you. The beauty of people of color is that we come in ALL shades. Some of our descendants from Africa, the Caribbean, and Spaniard countries have a hue of skin that is darker and some lighter than others."

Teresa further explains the beauty of her skin and the beauty of Chrissy's skin. "Melanin is an amazing pigment in our skin and hair that causes some of our skin to be darker and some of our skin to be lighter. Melanin helps fight against cancer, clears the skin, and makes you unique sweetie. So whenever you look in the mirror, always realize that your Melanin is Poppin'!"

The following day Chrissy goes back to daycare with a new understanding. Mrs. Sanchez approaches Chrissy and asks her, “How was your night? Did you learn anything new?”

Chrissy pulls out her new crayon box, which has 64 crayons, and takes out each shade of brown and tan she can find. She proudly answers, “My mommy is African American. I am too!"

"We, as African and Spanish descendants, come in a lot of shades, sizes, and colors. We should love each other no matter how dark or light our skin tone is," Chrissy explains.

Chrissy jumps for joy knowing that her black is beautiful.

After Chrissy's mother picked her up from daycare that day they celebrated their "Melanin Poppin'" over a cone of ice-cream.

The end...

...Actually it's just the beginning for a series to come.

NEXT BOOK

"Daddy, Why Do You Call Mommy Queen?"